AF472168

ESP's 9/11

by

Vito D'Angelo

AuthorHouse™
1663 Liberty Drive, Suite 200
Bloomington, IN 47403
www.authorhouse.com
Phone: 1-800-839-8640

First published by AuthorHouse 8/12/2008

ISBN: 978-1-4343-7051-8 (sc)

Printed in the United States of America
Bloomington, Indiana

This book is printed on acid-free paper.

It seems a great many people don't believe in future ESP. This is quite understandable; whenever they look to the future to find it, consciously there is nothing there yet. To have a much better idea of what your ESP sees in the future and far off in the future, <u>try looking constructively at what your ESP shows you of the past.</u> It shows something learned in the past to interpret what it sees in the future. Through ESP, I became aware that my conscious mind is just an observer and interpreter of the past and present time, projecting a future time as well.

To better communicate with each other, we try and do make common sense, and see common sense in things happening, which is good. I do it, but to recognize an ESP experience, you must be aware that ESP experiences usually make sense after you interpret them correctly. There are complications in ESP, because of names of people, language, and many different meanings to them. Don't misunderstand; I am not complaining. Also, ESP has follow-ups that make the same ESP experience go on for many years.. Correctly interpreted, ESP does make sense. **It answers questions I would want to know, care about in results of it as well**.

Through ESP, I understand better what happened to us on 9/11. I don't misunderstand our country's leaders, as it seems most others do, and what the future brings as a result of it. You will see in a few of my past ESP experiences how ESP helped me. Also, ESP literally saved my life by alerting me a few minutes beforehand. I mentioned the horror in this book, but can't bring myself to talk of it. A doctor said at the time that I survived it because I was alert, but I was alert because ESP alerted me within minutes of it. It's probably still on record from 1979. Other past experiences I had to show the accuracy of ESP that I will interpret with you can be proved to have happened as well.

This is not a fiction book; it is true, and as accurate as I can possibly interpret with you the way I see ESP and ESP's 9/11.

Extrasensory perception is believed to project the future. I believe it is the same part of my mind that helps me at the present time as well, providing me with **past reminder** pictures and little movies, which I narrowed down to two things. I am either getting **past reminders** helping me with everyday activities and things, or **past reminders** to interpret for future ESP.

I think of ESP as a nickname, like a partner, because it has been helpful to me at times for a long time. Since I was a young man, twenty-seven or twenty-eight, I was fascinated with future ESP. It has proven to be very accurate, as if it takes a picture of what happens long before it happens. Because it delivers in such a short time, like a flash of a light bulb on an old-fashioned camera, **sounds make names as well, and meanings are supported by actions and things as well. Most of the time, I have to interpret it; ESP seldom has time to explain.** One word like the run may have six or seven meanings to it, depending on what it shows me before, during, and after it. I have gotten future ESP experiences while doing anything awake, or while sleeping, or while waking from sleep. To give you a better understanding why I believe in it strongly, I have chosen the following ESP experiences, because I got them in a similar way to ESP's 9/11, which is from the major league of ESP, half-asleep, waking.

When I was about thirty-five years old, one morning in 1979, while waking from sleep, I heard the loud roar of a large aircraft directly over me. Without exaggeration, it sounded as loud as a plane the size of a 747, no more than forty feet over me. There were words not necessary to say, but it scared me as well. I got to my feet to check out the window; there was no aircraft in sight. Also, the nearest airport was too far away to hear them. **It was an**

ESP experience, but it scared me from taking a plane to go anywhere for about fifteen years, at age fifty. Only then did I take a plane again, because I trusted ESP for literally saving my life back in 1979 as well. ESP had warned me within minutes of the horrifying experience. Because ESP had shown me fifteen years later, it would be exciting for me to bowl on the Professional Senior Bowling Tour. As a result, I took two planes to, I think, St. Louis, to take a test for the touring professionals.

I went to practice for the tour at my friend's bowling lanes, and he said "Why are you bowling again?" I told him that I wanted to bowl with the Senior Professional Tour, and he said, "How are you going to do that? You have not bowled in fifteen or twenty years." I replied, "It's in my mind." Actually, I bowled about two or three years within sixteen or seventeen years.

I did well on tour. I saw my picture on television the very first tournament, placing within the top twenty-four professionals of two hundred bowlers.

10

It was most exciting, like a vacation recreation. And as many as two hundred professionals in every tournament! I got within the top twenty-four bowlers in about four or five tournaments out of nine. I had to give it up later on because of a knee injury at home, but it was great! Anyway, getting back to that morning in 1979, **and that loud aircraft sound, I believed to be ESP!**

A little later that morning, I was going to the racetrack, I think Belmont. I saw in the first race that the number ten horse was named Pet the Jet. Instantly I thought back at the ESP experience. I knew **Pet the Jet made the loud aircraft sound that I had gotten that morning.** Just by looking at the name—**a jet!** So that's what the loud sound was! I was positive it was, and it was going to win. Pet the Jet was a shipper. A shipper is a horse that comes from another racetrack. Pet the Jet came from Laurel and Bowie.

While I was looking at the racing form at the track and having coffee, a couple sat next to me. The man eventually asked me which horse I liked. "Ten horse. It's going to win. I am positive."

"What makes you so positive?" the man asked.

I did not want to talk about ESP, so I told him that horses coming from Laurel and Bowie racetracks run faster at this track. Then the man told his woman friend firmly, "That horse is not going to win. Don't bet it."

Then the woman turned to look me right in the eye. And I said, "Bet the horse." I could never forget the way she said "I will." Then I left the table and looked up at the odds board. The ten horse, Pet the Jet, was fifty to one, a long shot, to put it mildly.

I met my friend Frank, his friend, and their wives. I tried to convince them to bet it, but again, I could not bring myself to talk about ESP. Frank's friend bet a dollar on it, and I bet almost all the money in my pocket. The race started. Pet the Jet got the lead, and Frank said surprisingly, "He's got the lead."

Then I remember saying, "I told you he'll get the lead." The horses turned into the home stretch, and I told Frank, "Pet the Jet still has the lead."

Frank said, "I think he's gonna win." Pet the Jet was bet down the last minute or two, and paid $87 for every $2 bet. Even though the favorite won the second race, the daily double paid $599 for every $2 bet. When Pet the Jet had crossed that finish line clearly the winner, I jumped up and down two or three times. I don't think I tried to jump; it just happened. A black woman in front of me was pointing at my legs, laughing, having just as good a time looking at me jump as I was winning. There was more at stake than money. I walked a few steps to find the couple, but I saw the track was too crowded. I would never see them again, but I was satisfied that the woman bet it. She had said, "I will." Frank said he was short on money, which was why he could not bet the horse. I gave him money and left the track after hitting the daily double as well.

About the same time,1979, to get me to win another bet, ESP had me wake up with a deer's head on my pillow. My first reaction to it was *what's that?* I woke up on my stomach, looking at it, and I pulled myself up away from it as the head faded away. It was a very dark shadow with antlers. Later that day, my brother and I were about to bet on football when I saw the morning line. The Tampa Bay Buccaneers were either getting or giving eight points. Then I realized what I had woken up with that morning. Deer hunters referred to it as an eight-point buck. Yes! We won because the Buccaneers won.

Also, I want to talk about one other ESP experience that I had awakened with one morning before getting to ESP's 9/11. Like ESP's 9/11, it has distance. I didn't see the horse until seven years later.

In the year 2000, I saw at a racetrack a horse named **I Think. I Remembered It!** It was an ESP experience of seven years earlier, which I had done in front of my parents to show them in 1993. I was fifty years old. While waking, half-asleep and half-awake one morning, I saw myself standing with my arms stretched out and turning all around. In the ESP experience, my friend had said "Seven.". And **while turning around, I said, "I think the seven is going to win." Then my friend and I looked up at the clock and saw thirty-three seconds left.** Without trying to interpret it yet, I walked into my parents' home. They were sitting, and I did it in front them. Had I known what it meant, I would not have done it in front of them. Having seen the horse's name and number seven years later, in 2000, **I had no doubt that I Think, the number seven horse, was going to win. It turned out to be my biggest-money win ever. Because I knew there were threes in the ESP experience, I had won the pick three as well, two different times. I'm saying ESP saw the name and number of the horse seven years before it happened. I was fifty-seven years old when it won, and can prove it. I had to pay tax on the pick three. One pick three ending with a seven horse, paid fifty-to-one as well, It completed the pick three. I won money two different days that I saw it run.** I came to understand after interpreting ESP's 9/11 at age sixty-three that ESP was trying to get through to me back at age fifty. It was trying to have me interpret back then how long I will think and we, my parents as well, will think. **Because I did not know what the I Think ESP little movie experience meant back in 1993, I am unable to count the exact number of days my father left, about thirty-three days. I am fully aware why ESP wanted to bring this to my attention back at age fifty, and now is my first time talking about it. It would have been extremely helpful had I known at the time. I had learned long before this that ESP guides to the better way of a bad experience. The meaning of how long I will think goes far beyond the seven years already proven to me.** My purpose for sharing the "I Think" ESP little movie experience is to **make you aware** that ESP can **and does** see something or someone from at least the seven proven-to-me years before its happening. I stand by this a hundred percent.

I want to mention at this time that if I could make this kind of thing up, I would drop everything just to take up writing. I had very little in the way of an education, quitting school at age sixteen, only to go back later for one year of college. I only read newspapers and had written three essays in my entire life. One of these I gave to the college teacher who taught me, and the other two were for the Senior Professional Bowling Tour. To get on tour, I had to write two essays on a test. The looks of a typewriter made me feel insecure. I had not tried it in forty-seven years; I'm sixty-three.

Now, why would a guy who does not like reading and writing want to take this on? I kept forgetting what I wrote, and wasted a lot of writing. It took me more than eight months to write *ESP's 9/11.* When I had done the first paragraph and looked mentally ahead at it, my impression of it was that it's gonna require a professional writer. Copying from my own mind accurately to paper turned out to be a lot harder than I thought. I ignored the insecure feelings many times through it and moved on. I thought If I could only get close to the way I see *ESP's 9/11,* a professional writer might help. Well, I think I did get it accurately, otherwise I could not share it with you.

As I mentioned earlier, **I do get names and sounds that make names in my ESP little movie experiences.** Whenever I see psychics on television doing readings on someone, I wonder why they do so using initials. They would say to the person something like, "I get the initial L; who is that?" Then the person would say! I think the psychics on TV limit themselves when it comes to names. Also, I don't like the word *psychic,* even before I noticed that they talk to spirits, dead people. Otherwise, I am impressed. I believe they are getting their psychic info from the live person with whom they are talking. That is not to say that they don't believe in it. For me, I like ESP, and I believe it to be a loyal mental partner for the sensible good. Names of people and things usually are first to pick up on in my ESP.

I found ESP'S 9/11 to be something straight from the major leagues of ESP. I will never forget it. Here you can see ESP wants to communicate with me **about five hours before the actual attack. It shows me places and things that I had learned in the past, projecting the future.**

ESP's 9/11

ESP placed me in ***Country Club,*** *alongside of the* ***New England Thru-Way*** *and* ***Pelham Bay Park.*** *I was alone in Country Club, and it was dark. There was only a* ***large concrete stadium*** *which was about a block away in front of me, and a lot of concrete surface. Also,* ***big, tall snow piles, maybe twelve or fourteen feet high here and there*** *that only could have been made by* ***pushing snow with a snowplow.*** *Over* ***my right shoulder,*** *about a block and half away, was* ***a small bridge*** *that crossed from* ***Country Club*** *over to the other side,* ***Pelham Bay.*** *I thought* ***security*** *will* ***see us*** *that way. Then I looked to my left; it was dark. "This is the way to go," I said to my friend, who just came to me on my* ***right side.*** *He said, "Security will* ***see us*** *that way."* ***Then he raised his right hand, pointing*** *to the small bridge, saying, That's the way to go." Then I looked back to my left and saw a tremendous dark* ***dirty*** *white* ***snowstorm*** *covering houses, coming and coming fast. I was terrified and ran as fast as I could, the snow catching up to me from under and lifting me as I kept running. I kept thinking,* ***run up, keep running up***

the snow. *Daylight flashed on the snow, and the snow became white as* ***I kept thinking, keep running up the snow.*** *I ran all the way up the snow on a house roof, where I saw my friend again. He was standing on the edge of the roof with one foot and the other crossed it, leaning on its toe. The part of this I didn't get clear, was he seem to be leaning slightly on another like pointed roof. There was another house across the way, which was hardly in sight.* ***While pointing down off the front edge of the roof,*** *he called to men on the other house roof, saying* ***"If the snow covers us, you'll find us in here."*** *Then he stepped down about two feet to what seemed like a tar roof surface. He walked to the side of the roof and* ***walked down a long ladder,*** *and talked with two of his friends on the side of the house. The snowstorm ended before the ladder; there was no snow. I was too scared to walk down the ladder.*

I was half asleep, waking with ESP's 9/11, but I knew it to be ESP of some kind.

Mentally, I probably saw and wondered about the scary snowstorm about ten times or more. **I had never seen such a huge snowstorm,** but later that morning, I clicked on the television about 9 or 9:30. The two World Trade Center buildings were being attacked. And I knew within a minute of watching the attack, **Desert Storm** from Iraq was the cause of it. In ESP's 9/11, five hours earlier, a tremendous storm attacked, covering houses, and I wound up on one of two houses. On television, two buildings were being attacked. I knew the **storm that attacked houses and me was attacking the buildings on TV. Between the attack on TV and the way ESP had placed me in Country Club in ESP's 9/11**, **I knew we were <u>talking countries here</u>. The only country I knew that had a place named "storm" was Iraq—"Desert Storm."** Then I remembered, **we had a war there many years earlier. Saddam Hussein is the leader of Iraq.** I did not know the spelling of his name, so I told my family, "**Hoo-sane did it.**" I did not care to read about him, so I thought the **sound of his name, Hoo-sane, for five years.** The bulk of ESP's 9/11, the tremendous storm attack, is most powerful, judging from past ESP experiences like it.

Another telling sign that the attack had been ESP's 9/11: The people there had to **run up**town. **The two tall buildings were near the end of downtown Manhattan. In ESP's 9/11, I had to keep running up from a tremendous storm attack.** I had worked in the two World Trade Center buildings from time to time, and knew that the people had to **run uptown to get away from the two tall buildings being attacked.** The attack put mass transit out of commission and traffic at a standstill. As ESP's 911 had shone 5 hours before the 9/11 attack and since proved accurate. Keep running up for safety till you on Houston St.

As the people of our country watched in horror planes attacking our two buildings, I also saw a tremendous snowstorm attacking, which turned out to be Desert Storm in ESP's 9/11. The planes used to attack us on 9/11 were our own U.S. planes. At the time of the attack and still today, which is five and a half years later, I know of no other country in my mind that has, or had, a place named Storm but Iraq. My ESP has me interpret from what I know and what it means to me.

By projecting Desert Storm attacking us, ESP is saying that the attack came from Iraq and why. During the attack I knew that the U.S. had been in a war with the Iraq years before. Though I vaguely remember Desert Storm, to me it meant the war in Iraq. Back then, I remember U.S. troops with tanks fighting on a desert, and Iraq's troops surrending.

Like I mentioned, our own things were used to attack us. And I understand Bin Ladin went through a lot disguising his own Al Qaeda by making cells of them. Which still doe not hide who really had us attacked. ESP saw through it all!

Also, years later proved "**keep** running **up**town" to be **accurate** as well. About four or five years later, many thousands of people got sick with life-threatening illnesses from **white toxic dust** around the area, which is part of the reason **ESP showed dirty snowstorm attacking**. **The white toxic dust became part of the attack. People were covered in it.** Someone said on TV that about 10,000 people got sick and many died. There was no other way but to keep running uptown.

ESP, Snow, and Me. It was not solving who was responsible for attacking us that made ESP's 9/11 all that hard on me. A twist in it would make me wonder from time to time for more than five years, **why did ESP show me snow in its 9/11 little movie? A bad thing happened to us on 9/11. I felt bad, but snow means luck 4 to me in any ESP little movie. My mother used to play the numbers game when I was a kid. She used to say when she dreams snow, it means luck 4-o. I played horses, so for me, snow meant the number four horse will win; it did win. Snow means luck 4 of something in every little ESP movie. ESP shows me a tremendous dark, dirty white snowstorm attacking me in its 9/11 little movie. I was terrified, light flashed, and the snow turned white. I did not see in the 9/11 attack luck 4 of something. It seemed to me at the time that ESP could have used another kind of storm to have me interpret Desert Storm. I did not comprehend, even though I was aware that ESP projects what it sees.** Well, it took more than five years for me to realize. ESP could not use another kind of storm to interpret Desert Storm **with**

involvements to my surprise and amazement. Had it not been for snow in ESP's 9/11, I would have stopped trying to solve it the moment I found out where the attack was coming from.

I wondered from time to time for more than five years, what was four of something in ESP's 9/11 that will win or turn to luck for my country. I could have never spotted the reason for snow in ESP's 9/11 more than five years later if I were not thinking of it from time to time.. Despite not wanting to talk about ESP in the past, finding the reason for snow in ESP's 9/11, I felt compelled to write this book. I felt it was the only way to have ESP's 9/11 told in its entirety.

Two of my friends escaped from the tall buildings. They talked of how it was there. I felt both sad and angry, and I could not wait for our country's leaders to get payback.

President Bush blamed Bin Ladin for the 9/11 attack, and he was asking the Afghani people to turn him over to the U.S. They did not do it, and our country went to war. The country of England, our true pals, fought on our side against Bin Ladin and Afghanistan. England had lost about forty or forty-two of its own in the attack.

I want to mention at this time that England is shown in ESP' s 9/11 as true pals five hours before the attack and proved accurate after.

I wondered why President Bush was going after Bin Ladin. **Saddam Hoo-sane did it**. I had not interpreted much of ESP's 9/11 yet. Later I did see Bin Ladin in it also.

Things about the man on the roof in ESP's 9/11 that I kept going over mentally: He was standing on the front edge of the house roof with one foot, the other crossed it on its toe, and he was leaning on another like pointed roof while he was **pointing down off the roof's front edge.** He called to men on the other house, **"If the snow covers us, you will find us in here."** Then he stepped down off the edge, walked to the side of the roof, and walked down a ladder. Then he talked with two men on the side of the house where snow did not get to. I was too scared to walk down the ladder.

I felt there had to be a meaning to it. It was too common for a ladder to be on the side of a house. **Finally!** I unstymied myself when I asked the right question. What has the man been doing when **he stepped off the ladder to talk to two men on the side of the house?** The answer gave me **the <u>sound</u> of the man's name! He's been ladden;** again, the sound of the answer gave me the man's name: "**He's <u>Bin Ladin</u>**." The ladder is on the side of the house with two of his pals which means Bin Ladin and his people were on Iraq's side. It shows Bin Ladin and his people to be on Iraq's side in a similar way the country of England was on the U.S.'s side after the attack against Afghanistan, except Bin Ladin and Hussein proved to be sneaky, dirty. And my being too scared to walk down the ladder definitely reflects Bin Ladin's feelings. He's too scared to come out from hiding, maybe scared of going down in rank as well. Also, ESP had me do Hussein, but run in Bin Ladin's place up on the house to learn more about him, gauge

If the snow covers us, you'll find us in here.

better, and learn more about ESP's 9/11. I ran in Bin Ladin's place because I did what Bin Ladin had to do and wound up there with him to interpret him and things. What's ESP trying to tell me? Note: ESP does not have to explain to me that Bin Ladin is the boss of Al Qaeda; ESP little movies happened like flash, within seconds. I have to interpret what I see most of the time and the meaning to me. Even though I learned the name sound Al Qaeda after this ESP little movie, it does not matter. It is ESP, and one of the great many ways in which it works.

I believe ESP also let me run in Bin Ladin's place to have me interpret that he is hiding in Iran. It makes sense to me from this part of ESP's 9/11. Since 9/11, he became more of a man on the run, but I don't see him run. Bin Ladin had to run up the house, as I did, because he started with me in the same place in Iraq. He had pointed to the bridge, which is the only way to go right before the tremendous snowstorm attack. No other way can go right. I only see him again on the house's roof, which tells me that ESP wanted me to get the past sense of I run, which is I ran. He pointed where he was going, which was the bridge on the right, and I ran in his place. Had I seen Bin Ladin run, the past tense would have been "he ran," thus unable to make connection, **Iran.** Remember, I discovered Bin Ladin in ESP's 9/11 in past tense of what he was doing, to learn more about him. He did not run in ESP's 9/11. **I ran.** Which may be **a**nother reason ESP scared me from going down ladder, the past tense would have been I or We ladden. Also, **Bin Ladin makes it past the snow time period, which will become clear to you later.**

I knew nothing about their countries and names. They were too foreign for me to remember, but I wanted to know where Iran and Iraq was. I asked the librarian for a world map, but he handed me an atlas. I saw from the position Hussein and Bin Ladin first started in Iraq that Iran is to the right. Before this, I did not have a clue where Iran was. So now I not only have past tense giving me Iran, I have Bin Ladin pointing right there. Iran on the map looks like a neighbor of Iraq on the right.

As mentioned, Bin Ladin had pointed off the front edge of house roof, which turned out to be the exact spot U.S. troops would find Hussein two years after the 9/11 attack. I saw it on TV news. **U.S. troops uncovered** a hole about twenty or thirty feet in front of a white or light tan house to find him. Hussein looked up at them, and U.S. troops looked down at him, like thinking, *look what we found!* I did not realize at the time that Bin Ladin had been saying where to find Hussein in his complex sentence, <u>**which is the same sentence ESP made him say to have me interpret.**</u> I found out three years later, which made it five years after the attack, by finding the understood sound **Hussin** for **Hussein** in Bin Ladin's complex sentence. This told me a lot, but it was five years after the 9/11 attack.

First, I want to point out that the two country leaders started in Iraq in ESP's 9/11 before the Desert Storm attack. Hussein was **still alone, looking for a way to get by security without being seen**. Then his pal Bin Ladin came up on **his right side**, was sure that he had the right way without being seen by security .They were not discussing a left or right turn. They were planning an attack, looking for a right way to get by security, and as well, **get away with it for themselves**. The two countries' leaders did not want take any chances, and met while dark in Iraq. All this shows planning of what came next, **the tremendous Storm attack from Iraq on 9/11. Which I can only interpret the name of storm to be Desert Storm in ESP's 9/11..** Also, it shows Bin Ladin **running to** where **he raised his right hand pointing** before the attack—a small bridge, which is the only way to go right. Bin Ladin ran from the snowstorm attack, 9/11, but **I ran for him.** Bin Ladin went the right way for him, I believe to Iran, and Hussein turned left again, left of where Bin Ladin ran. He was captured two years later by U.S. troops about twenty or thirty feet in front of a white house. I did not see either one of them while running up the snow in ESP's 9/11, so the two country leaders as well did not see each other after 9/11. ESP let me run in Bin Ladin's place as well to show me he ran to Iran, but two years after 9/11, not before. When Hussein was found two years after 9/11 by U.S. troops, Bin Ladin made it to Iran at the same time, which will be better understood in Bin Ladin's complex sentence later. Also, **Bin Ladin makes it over or past the snow time period which will be clear to you later as well.**

It was September 2006, which was five years after the 9/11 attack. I was reading the newspapers and saw Saddam Hussein was on trial in Iraq. For the first time, I took a good look at the spelling of his name. His name was not as I thought at all, which was Hoo-sane. The sound was different. It had a **Huss in** sound to me. So I mentally searched ESP's 9/11 for a sound like Hussin. Yes! I found the name; it is in Bin Ladin's complex sentence showing its meaning and occurrences as well. Bin Ladin had been pointing to the very spot where U.S. troops did find Hussein, which made the sentence's meaning understood. **The name sound Hussin with no E is understood in the sentence because Desert Storm from Iraq attacked as a snowstorm.** ESP would have shown Hussin's name sound as I knew it, which is **Hoo-sane**, but could not without a misinterpretation. **US in the sentence stands for U.S. and forms the sound Huss**

to show the correct meanings. The house across the way stands for U.S. White House, not Bin Ladin's friend's house. Remember, we are talking countries here. Again, Bin Ladin's complex sentence, but adjusted to show the capture with Hussein two years after 9/11. **"If the snow covers U.S., you will find Hussin here." U.S. troops did find Hussein there, so Bin Ladin had to be talking to the U.S. White House across the way. The word <u>us as well</u> means Huss, with words sounding Huss and in combined in the sentence are understood to form Hussin for Hussein. I had seen it on TV two years after the attack. U.S. troops did find Hussein in front of a tan or white house, which was where Bin Ladin had pointed, making the sentence's meanings understood. It's hard to talk about, but it is unbelievably accurate; it happened.**

Again, Bin Ladin's complex sentence at first meaning tells his pals where to find him: "If the snow covers <u>us,</u> you'll find **<u>us in</u>** here." Two years later, the same sentence adjusted to a happening connected the snowstorm attack with those involved.

Hussein was found by the **U.S.** where Bin Ladin pointed, saying to them they would. "If the **snow covers U.S., you'll** find **Hussin** here. **"The snow covered U.S. from Desert Storm attack on 9/11. Sentence changes are understood at the time. U.S. people were covered on 9/11 because of Desert Storm.**

The word **If** in Bin Ladin's complex sentence proves to me again that ESP does a great deal more than take pictures of what it sees in the future. **If** is used to show happenings with those involved and adjust the time period, which will be explained later. **If** shows Hussein was responsible because the U.S. was really covered and Hussein was really found in hole front of house. Therefore, Hussein was responsible for the covering, **and ESP is only showing what is involved and who.** We already learned Bin Ladin was on his side. Also, the sentence shows and means men from the U.S. White House **went to Iraq to find Hussein for the covering**. The adjusted sentence: **"If the snow covers U.S., you'll find Hussin here."** Again, part of the meaning of the sentence shows men from the U.S. White House went to Iraq to find Hussein for the covering of 9/11.Only the U.S. White House could send men to find Hussein for the Desert Storm attack on 9/11. Hussein was found by U.S. troops.

After realizing the name Hussein had been in Bin Ladin's complex sentence, in ESP's 9/11. I believed for a short while that Press Secretary Tony Snow had something to do with time periods, but I dismissed it**. I remembered the U.S. White House had a different press secretary at the time of Hussein's capture. I was disappointed. Tony Snow would have explained snow in ESP's 9/11 because it's a name connecting someone involved, or connecting something involved.** I thought of calling the FBI just to confirm it. Then I thought they would only wonder what I was up to and if I were honest with them by telling them about ESP, they would think me crazy. I believed Tony Snow was not the U.S. White House press secretary at time **Hussein was uncovered by U.S. troops in front of a house, <u>which was another reason my thinking Tony Snow's time period then did not work. I did not realize it at the time, but I needed Hussein to</u>**

be covered by the U.S. to add Tony Snow's time period to the meaning of Bin Ladin's complex sentence as well. I was disappointed again, not having found the reason for snow in ESP's 9/11, but I did not anticipate three months later.

December 29, five years and three months after 9/11,finally I realized that snow has something to do with a name. The name belongs to White House Press Secretary Tony Snow, and is used to show different time periods, involvement, meanings, and results of them. President Bush had replaced another press secretary for Tony Snow sometime after the capture of Hussein, which made Tony Snow's time period a factor. I don't know how long after the capture Tony Snow was appointed. And I had not heard of him before the appointment.

December 29,2006.

What other place but the Internet, which connects the U.S. states, would ESP show me **reasons for snow in ESP's 9/11?** Also,I'm new to the Internet, and got Pogo in June. I was playing Pogo Bowl on the

Internet about 4 or 5 am when I saw chatter. "Hey, did you hear about **Hussin**?" For the first time ever, I saw the **name Hussin sounded the way I had learned it in Bin Ladin's complex sentence recently in September, with no E in it.** The chat continued: "Do you think there would be any problems because of it?" After he said *problems because of it,* I turned on the radio news. Yes, the Iraqis hanged Hussein the previous night, which told me what snow's **meanings are in ESP's 9/11**.One of which is **Hussein will covered at the time period of Tony Snow in U.S. White House. And snow had been projected connecting all involved from the beginning to end, showing what, why and who attacked us. The end showing results with Tony Snow for U.S. White House involvement, and his name snow meaning to me reflecting country wise results. I was amazed! ESP HAD JUSTIFIED SNOW IN ITS 9/11! I knew ESP had to see the name Hussin on the U.S. Internet to project it before the 9/11 attack. ESP had to have seen the name Hussin on the Internet to go accordingly and accurately to the time period Hussein covered. Which is the**

Tony Snow time period.. ESP had won me over again. I saw for the first time ever, the spelling sound Hussin at the exact same time I learned he was covered. Tony Snow's last name was part of the reason ESP projected a snow Desert Storm attacking us, connecting snow to those involved, projecting results as well. It was chilling the way ESP used the **word IF** in Bin Ladin's complex sentence, showing the **time period Hussin to be covered. "If the snow covers Huss, you'll find U.S. in here." Meaning Hussein is caught by his own snowstorm plan and covered at the Tony Snow time period, and you can find U.S. in Iraq.** The U.S. had taken over Iraq. There were other reasons **Hussein was covered. The main reason, according to ESP, was for covering U.S. citizens on 9/11. And based on my past experience with ESP, to me it is a fact, especially the way ESP had connected snow to the U.S. White House involvement with Bin Ladin, pointing to where they would find Hussein and finally, when Hussein covered. The name connecting those involved would have been enough to explain snow in ESP's 9/11. But, as**

mentioned in ESP's 9/11, daylight flashed and the snow turned white. Tony Snow's time period, and his name being Snow projected for its meaning to me as well, reflects the future relationship for the four countries involved, country-wise results as projected before the attack.

As you recall in ESP's 9/11 Country Club, snow had been pushed, resulting in big, tall snow piles in a lot to the concrete stadium in Country Club. Alongside Country Club was **Pelham Bay and the New England Thru-Way** which means **Pal'em countries** = **Pal them countries**. England, our true pals, fought on our side after the attack, making us two countries. The two pal terrorist country leaders make two countries as well, **a total of four countries.** Even though I had seen snow piles already made before the snowstorm attack, it obviously shows the time period after the snowstorm attack for success. **Even though I do not see the name Afghanistan in ESP's 9/11, I am assured of a fourth pal country relationship. ESP projected snow, meaning 4 to**

me. We were attacked mainly from the country of Iraq.

The snow piles are in Country Club that is Iraq in ESP's 9/11. It means Iraq is the fourth and final country. Iraq is country pal number 4, and ESP really proved to be correct! Again, ESP projected before the attack. That Iraq would be country pal number 4. At the time period starting with Tony Snow in the U.S. White House.

The snow piles, meaning pals, had been pushed, which reflects how they are made, not voluntary. I'll not say this four pal country-wise relationship will be for a great many years. **ESP shows better than that.** The four pal country-wise relationship will have a **concrete stay for the future.**

Even though I don't see the name of the country Afghanistan in ESP's 9/11, I am assured of a fourth pal country relationship by projecting snow in Country Club. Therefore I must include Afghanistan to make four countries involved in ESP's 9/11. It also was the country U.S. and England fought side by side just after 9/11.

Five and a half years after the 9/11 attack, I felt like seeing the concrete stadium, because it is in ESP's 9/11. I have not been there in about thirty-five years.

The concrete stadium has meanings, **one of which is Desert Storm.** It shows in ESP's 9/11 to be the only place within Country Club, meaning a place within a country, **and is made of sand. It's made of sand not only to me; it actually is made of sand!** From sand, cement was made and dried, resulting in a **rock concrete stadium = Desert Storm from Iraq!**

The concrete stadium is in Country Club which a real place three miles from my home. I have not been there to see it for about thirty five years. I did not think about it, obviously to me, ESP projected Country Club to do countries. The Concrete stadium verifies the tremendous storm to be Desert Storm!

Desert Storm was in Iraq therefore confirming Country Club to be Iraq in ESP's 9/11. The bridge over my right shoulder in Country Club goes Pelham Bay. Pelham Bay on the right side over the bridge represents their pal country. Crossing the bridge in Country Club is the only way to go right! And going right from Iraq, country wise, leads to Iran. An Atlas map confirms it. It confirms to me as well, ESP projected Hussein and Bin Ladin in Iraq accurately! Remember, I interpreted Iran in ESP's 9/11 before I knew where it was.

If you had a hard time believing what I said so far, I could imagine what you would think of this. Which is true as well. ESP projected me in its Country Club 9/11, 2001. That actually happened in March, 2007. I have no other explanation for it. I did not realize it at the time, but I did get kind of wary in Country Club.

I walked across the small bridge from the Pelham Bay side, looking left for it. I did not see it, and made a left after crossing the bridge. I walked about a block and a half. **Then I simulated like in ESP's 9/11** turning, so I could look at the small bridge over my right shoulder. Then I looked in front of me for the concrete stadium, but there were rows of private family houses. In ESP's 9/11, there were only the concrete stadium and big, tall snow piles on the concrete surface from the stadium to me and around the lot. A man was having a smoke outside his house, and I asked him "Is this Country Club?" He said yes. I said, "I'm looking for the concrete stadium." He said that was torn down many years ago, then **he raised his right hand, pointing** about another three blocks left.

I became aware that he raised his right hand pointing like Bin Ladin in ESP'9/11. Bin Ladin pointed about the same spot but to the bridge. The man was like saying, go that way then go right. And there was no one else, we were the only two, as in ESP'9/11.

He said as I was about to walk away that the name was Rice Stadium. As I turned left, walking away from him, the name stuck in my mind—Rice Stadium.

I did not know the concrete stadium was named Rice, which made me think of Condoleezza Rice. She replaced someone in the U.S. White House, and like Tony Snow, I don't remember when. His name is Colin Powell, who was in the Desert Storm war as well. I don't remember the name of the person Tony Snow replaced. I got to where the stadium used to be, and I asked another man. Yes, he remembered it torn down about ten to twelve years ago. Then I asked if he remembered the name of the concrete stadium. He said yes, **Rice!**

Well, it's like I said earlier: ESP had shown me places and things to see the future before the attack more than five years ago. The concrete stadium stands for Desert Storm in ESP's 9/11,and an important person named Rice is in the U.S. White House. I don't think it to be a coincidence. I believe ESP is just doing what it does best, connecting those and what's involved to show the future. Now I find ESP had projected before the 9/11 attack, the name Rice to the concrete stadium that is Desert Storm in ESP's 9/11. Five and a half years after ESP's 9/11, let's get real. Is the U.S. in Iraq? Is Iraq the fourth pal country? As well, does the U.S. White House have someone there named Rice? All of the ESP that I have written is true and accurate. To accuse me of making this up would be to accuse me of being brilliant, which is not so with my education. It is impossible for me to make this all up. The truth is, I'm just interpreting from ESP as accurately as I possibly can. I had to walk past the small bridge on my way back home. It looked the same way it did in ESP's 9/11. Knowing ESP has follow-ups, I could not help feeling a little wary walking past the small bridge, hoping I'd be okay. Also, I have not been to the concrete stadium in about thirty-five years. Had it not been for ESP **wanting to have me to interpret its 9/11, and what the future would bring from its 9/11**, I probably would not have thought of this place again. And that desert storm is here to stay.

Because I know ESP usually has follow-ups, I had been concerned about huge storms after ESP's 9/11. I didn't keep dates, but they caused people to go to the roofs of their houses. The storm that most resembled the tremendous snowstorm attack in ESP's 9/11 is the tsunami, which a gigantic wave covered houses caused by a tremendous storm. There were other storms. Sometime after Hussein was covered, I observed a huge snow and ice storm in January.

When I heard of it, it already traveled through about nine or ten U.S states and was still going. In early February, it seemed like the same storm, a snow and ice storm, was traveling through U.S. states. Then in April, would you believe, about April 15, a snow and rain storm kept traveling through U.S. states. I first heard of it in Texas. It traveled southeast, then got to me in the east and past me to upstate New York. They called it a Nor'easter because it traveled east.

Thank you, reader.
—Vito D'Angelo

www.ingramcontent.com/pod-product-compliance
Ingram Content Group UK Ltd.
Pitfield, Milton Keynes, MK11 3LW, UK
UKHW040020200726
13854UKWH00001B/280